Courtesy of Museum of Fine Arts, Boston

Painting titled *Portrait of Samuel Adams* by John Singleton Copley – Adams points at the Massachusetts Charter, which he regarded as a document that protected the rights of the people – 1722

STANDARDS-BASED LEARNING & FUN!

FOUNDING FATHERS

Primary Sources

ACADEMICS' CHOICE™ SMART BOOK AWARD WINNER

20 Primary Sources!
We dug through the archives so you don't have to!

TEACH IT TODAY! CORE RESOURCE™

by Carole Marsh

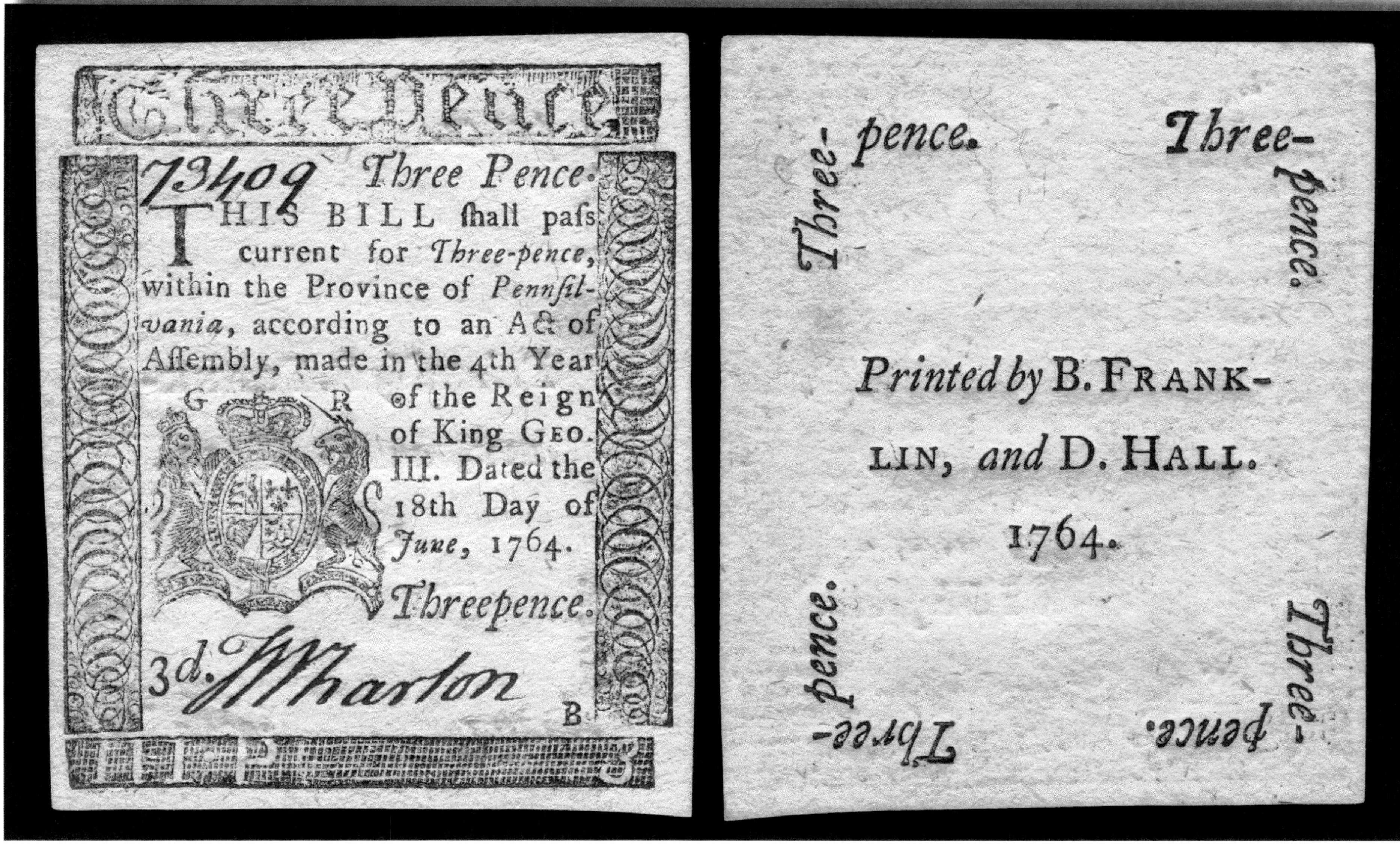

Courtesy of Wikimedia Commons

Photograph of three-pence Pennsylvania colonial currency printed by Benjamin Franklin – 1764

Courtesy of Museum of Fine Arts, Boston

Painting titled *Portrait of John Hancock* by John Singleton Copley – 1765

The Second Day of July 1776, will be the most memorable Epocha, in the History of America.

I am apt to believe that it will be celebrated, by succeeding Generations, as the great anniversary Festival. It ought to be commemorated, as the Day of Deliverance by solemn Acts of Devotion to God Almighty. It ought to be solemnized with Pomp and Parade, with Shews, Games, Sports, Guns, Bells, Bonfires and Illuminations from one End of this Continent to the other from this Time forward forever more.

You will think me transported with Enthusiasm but I am not. -- I am well aware of the Toil and Blood and Treasure, that it will cost Us to maintain this Declaration, and support and defend these States. -- Yet through all the Gloom I can see the Rays of ravishing Light and Glory. I can see that the End is more than worth all the Means. And that Posterity will tryumph in that Days Transaction, even altho We should rue it, which I trust in God We shall not.

Courtesy of Adams Family Papers, Massachusetts Historical Society

Transcript of the last few paragraphs of a letter from John Adams to his wife, discussing America's Declaration of Independence – July 3, 1776

Courtesy of Library of Congress

Engraved print of Benjamin Franklin, envoy from the American Congress to the French court – 1780

Text translates to: **In this building, once Hotel of York, on September 3, 1783, David Hartly, in the name of the King of England, Benjamin Franklin, John Jay, John Adams, in the name of the United States of America, signed the Definite Peace Treaty recognizing the independence of the United States.**

Courtesy of Wikimedia Commons

Photograph of plaque commemorating the Treaty of Paris ending the American Revolution – 1783

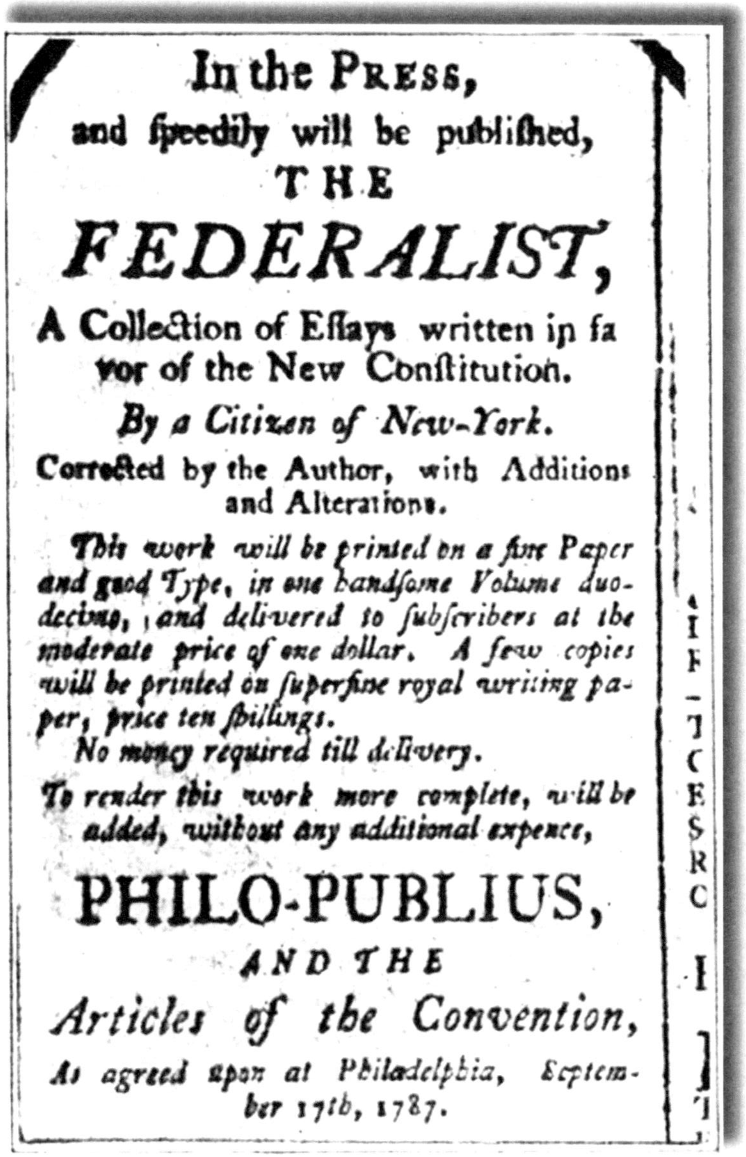

In the PRESS,
and ſpeedily will be publiſhed,
THE
FEDERALIST,
A Collection of Eſſays written in favor of the New Conſtitution.
By a Citizen of New-York.
Corrected by the Author, with Additions and Alterations.

This work will be printed on a fine Paper and good Type, in one handſome Volume duodecimo, and delivered to ſubſcribers at the moderate price of one dollar. A few copies will be printed on ſuperfine royal writing paper, price ten ſhillings.

No money required till delivery.

To render this work more complete, will be added, without any additional expence,

PHILO-PUBLIUS,
AND THE
Articles of the Convention,
As agreed upon at Philadelphia, September 17th, 1787.

An advertisement for *The Federalist*– 1787

Courtesy of Project Gutenberg

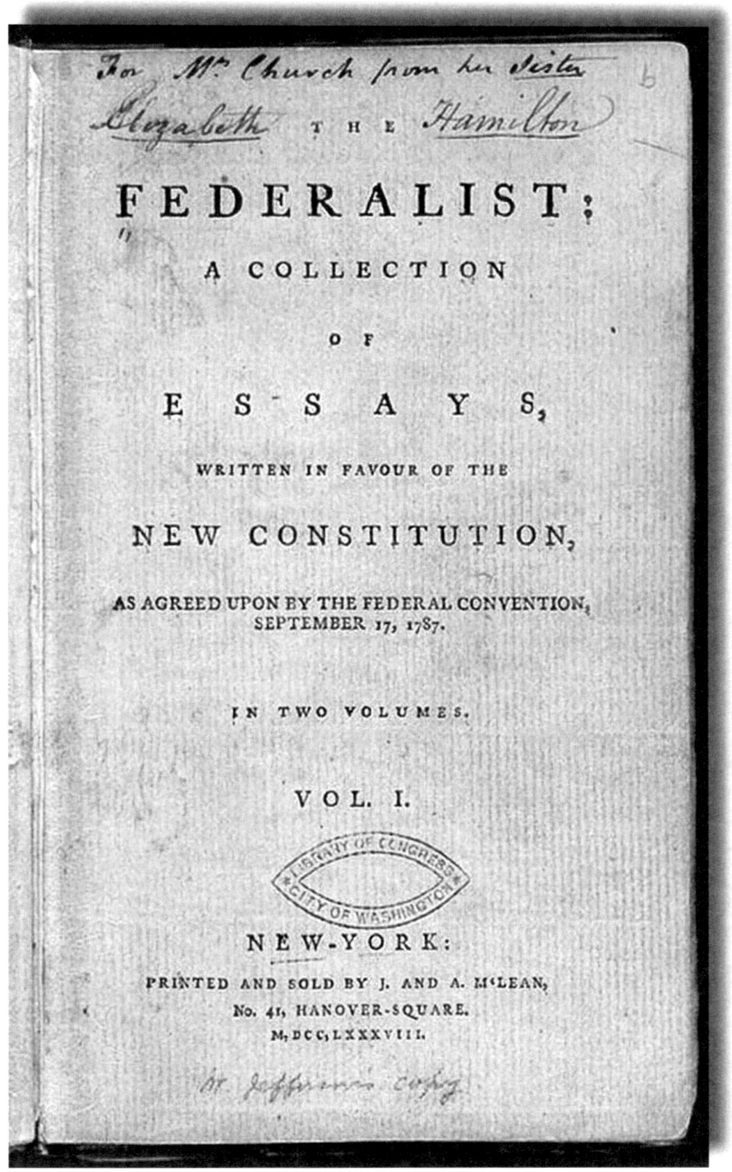

For Mrs Church from her Sister Elizabeth Hamilton

THE
FEDERALIST:
A COLLECTION
OF
ESSAYS,
WRITTEN IN FAVOUR OF THE
NEW CONSTITUTION,
AS AGREED UPON BY THE FEDERAL CONVENTION, SEPTEMBER 17, 1787.
IN TWO VOLUMES.
VOL. I.

NEW-YORK:
PRINTED AND SOLD BY J. AND A. M'LEAN,
No. 41, HANOVER-SQUARE.
M,DCC,LXXXVIII.

Title page of the first collection of *The Federalist*– 1788

Courtesy of Library of Congress

Documents related to *The Federalist*– collection of 85 articles and essays written under the pseudonym "Publius" by Alexander Hamilton, James Madison, and John Jay to promote the ratification of the U.S. Constitution

Courtesy of the Bureau of Engraving and Printing

Engraved portrait of Alexander Hamilton, first U.S. Secretary of the Treasury – circa 1789

Courtesy of the White House Historical Association

Portrait of Thomas Jefferson – 1800

Portrait of James Madison – "Father of the Constitution" – 1816

Courtesy of the White House Historical Association

Photograph of presidential $1 coin featuring James Madison – photo taken 2007

Courtesy of U.S. Mint

Portrait of James Madison and photo of presidential coin featuring his likeness

Courtesy of Philadelphia Museum of Art

Painting titled *Benjamin Franklin Drawing Electricity from the Sky*– circa 1816

Courtesy of Library of Congress

Painting titled *Declaration of Independence* by John Trumbull – 1817

Courtesy of Virginia Museum of Fine Arts

Painting titled *Washington as Farmer at Mount Vernon* by Junius Brutus Stearns – depicts George Washington on his Mount Vernon property – famous home is seen in the background – 1851

Courtesy of Library of Congress

Lithographic print of painting titled *Give Me Liberty, or Give Me Death*– depicts the famous speech made by Patrick Henry in 1775 – print circa 1876

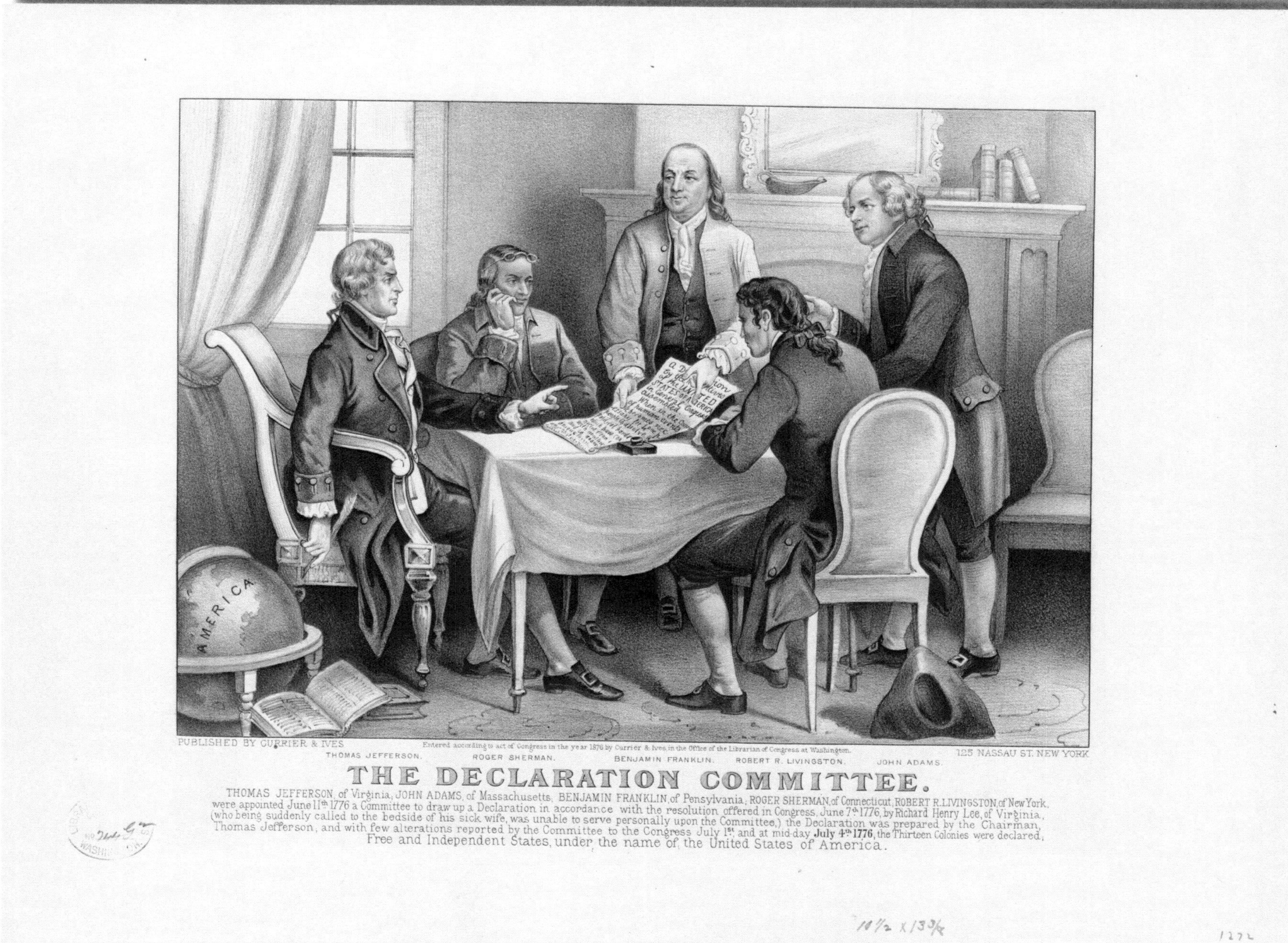

Courtesy of Library of Congress

Print showing members of the Declaration of Independence committee – from left to right: Thomas Jefferson, Roger Sherman, Benjamin Franklin, Robert R. Livingston, and John Adams – 1876

Courtesy of New York Public Library

Lithograph depicting George Washington, Patrick Henry, and Edmund Pendleton traveling from Virginia to the First Continental Congress in Philadelphia – 1886

Courtesy of National Numismatic Collection at the Smithsonian Institution

Photograph of $100 silver certificate, Series of 1891, featuring James Monroe

Courtesy of Library of Congress

**Painting titled *The Birth of Old Glory* by Percy Moran –
depicts Betsy Ross showing an American flag to George Washington – circa 1917**

Courtesy of U.S. Navy

Photograph showing stern view of destroyer USS *John Hancock* – 1981

Photograph of the Assembly Room in Independence Hall (Philadelphia, Pennsylvania) – the Continental Congress declared American independence in this room in 1776 – photo taken 2011

FOUNDING FATHERS

Primary Sources

Historical Documents • Maps • Photographs • Political Cartoons

INCLUDES 20 PRIMARY SOURCE DOCUMENTS:

- Painting titled *Portrait of Samuel Adams* by John Singleton Copley – Adams points at the Massachusetts Charter, which he regarded as a document that protected the rights of the people – 1722
- Photograph of three-pence Pennsylvania colonial currency printed by Benjamin Franklin – 1764
- Painting titled *Portrait of John Hancock* by John Singleton Copley – 1765
- Transcript of the last few paragraphs of a letter from John Adams to his wife, discussing America's Declaration of Independence – July 3, 1776
- Engraved print of Benjamin Franklin, envoy from the American Congress to the French court – 1780
- Photograph of plaque commemorating the Treaty of Paris ending the American Revolution – 1783
- Documents related to *The Federalist* – collection of 85 articles and essays written under the pseudonym "Publius" by Alexander Hamilton, James Madison, and John Jay to promote the ratification of the U.S. Constitution
- Engraved portrait of Alexander Hamilton, first U.S. Secretary of the Treasury – circa 1789
- Portrait of Thomas Jefferson – 1800
- Portrait of James Madison and photo of presidential coin featuring his likeness
- Painting titled *Benjamin Franklin Drawing Electricity from the Sky* – circa 1816
- Painting titled *Declaration of Independence* by John Trumbull – 1817
- Painting titled *Washington as Farmer at Mount Vernon* by Junius Brutus Stearns – depicts George Washington on his Mount Vernon property – famous home is seen in the background – 1851
- Lithographic print of painting titled *Give Me Liberty, or Give Me Death* – depicts the famous speech made by Patrick Henry in 1775 – print circa 1876
- Print showing members of the Declaration of Independence committee – from left to right: Thomas Jefferson, Roger Sherman, Benjamin Franklin, Robert R. Livingston, and John Adams – 1876
- Lithograph depicting George Washington, Patrick Henry, and Edmund Pendleton traveling from Virginia to the First Continental Congress in Philadelphia – 1886
- Photograph of $100 silver certificate, Series of 1891, featuring James Monroe
- Painting titled *The Birth of Old Glory* by Percy Moran – depicts Betsy Ross showing an American flag to George Washington – circa 1917
- Photograph showing stern view of destroyer USS *John Hancock* – 1981
- Photograph of the Assembly Room in Independence Hall (Philadelphia, Pennsylvania) – the Continental Congress declared American independence in this room in 1776 – photo taken 2011

Perfect for Gallery Walks & Literature Circles!

Build Higher-Order Thinking Skills:

- Analysis
- Critical Thinking
- Point of View
- Compare and Contrast
- Order of Events
- & Much More!

FREE 15-page Online Teacher's Guide!
www.gallopade.com/pstg

GALLOPADE

www.gallopade.com
Printed in Peachtree City, GA

ISBN-13: 978-0-635-13161-4 $17.99